UFO Sighting!

Suddenly a blinding beam of light shot down from the sky. Bert crouched and pressed his hands over his eyes. But he couldn't shut out the light.

Then, just as suddenly, the light vanished. Bert looked up—and gasped. Just overhead, so close he could almost touch it, was a circle of colored lights. The lights turned slowly at first, then more rapidly. The silence was eerie.

With a faint *whoosh,* the circle of lights flew up. It disappeared behind a line of trees.

"Wow!" Bert whispered. "I don't believe it! I think I just saw a UFO!"

Books in The New Bobbsey Twins series

Available from MINSTREL Books

THE NEW
Bobbsey
Twins™

#5
THE CASE OF
THE CLOSE
ENCOUNTER

LAURA LEE HOPE
ILLUSTRATED BY PAUL JENNIS

A
MINSTREL®
BOOK

PUBLISHED BY POCKET BOOKS

New York   London   Toronto   Sydney   Tokyo   Singapore

A MINSTREL PAPERBACK *ORIGINAL*

 A Minstrel Book published by
POCKET BOOKS, a division of Simon & Schuster, Inc.,
1230 Avenue of the Americas, New York, N.Y. 10020

Produced by Mega-Books of New York, Inc.

ISBN: 0-671-62656-6

First Minstrel Books printing April 1988

10 9 8 7 6 5 4 3 2

Contents

THE CASE OF
THE CLOSE
ENCOUNTER

1
Look! Up in the Sky!

Bert Bobbsey groaned.

Flossie and Freddie giggled.

Mrs. Bobbsey glanced in the rearview mirror. "Don't tease Bert, kids. It's nice of him to fill in for Nan."

"I wasn't teasing, Mom," said Flossie. "Was I, Bert?"

"Telling the truth isn't teasing," Flossie's twin, Freddie, said. "Nan says Artie Houlihan gets into lots of trouble. More than any other kid she sits for."

Bert's twin sister, Nan, was a baby-sitter for the Houlihans' five-year-old son. "I can handle him," twelve-year-old Bert said. "I've been looking after you two for years. I'm an expert with troublemakers."

Earlier that day, Nan had come home sick from school. At dinnertime she'd felt even sicker. And she was supposed to be at the Houlihans' by seven-fifteen.

"It's too late for them to find another sitter," Nan had said to Bert. "Will you, as a special favor, please take my place?"

Now Bert wondered if he'd made a mistake. Would Artie be as bad as everyone said?

"Maybe he'll tie you to a chair," Freddie said. "I saw that in a cartoon."

Flossie sniffed. "That's dopey," she said. "Things in cartoons don't really happen."

"Oh yeah? What about—?"

"Hold it," Bert said. "Artie and I are going to have fun. He's not going to do anything he isn't supposed to."

"I know a game we can play," Artie said. He jumped up on the sofa and his foot kicked a box of crayons to the floor. Half of the crayons rolled under the sofa.

"What game?" Bert asked.

Artie bounced up and down. He said, "It's called stop-and-goky-oky-choky."

"Oh, sure," said Bert. "That's one of my favorite games. How do we play it?"

"It's easy. When you say stop, we stop. And when I say go, we go."

"What about the oky-choky part?"

Artie stopped bouncing. "That's different," he said. "When I say 'oky-choky,' you turn around and count to ten. That's what oky-choky means."

"What about when *I* say 'oky-choky'?"

"You can't," Artie said. "Only one person in the game can say oky-choky. It's a rule."

Bert smiled. "Okay," he said. "Let's pick up the crayons first."

"We can't. That's not part of the game."

"Artie. . . !"

"GO!" shouted Artie. He ran toward the stairs.

"Wait a minute!" Bert dashed after him. He'd never seen a little kid run so fast. "Artie, come back here! Stop!"

Artie froze four steps up. Grinning, he looked down at Bert. Then he frowned. "You're moving," he complained. "When you say 'stop,' we both have to stop. It's a rule."

Bert stood still. "Sorry," he said. "I—"

"Go!"

Artie was all the way up the stairs before Bert called out, "Stop!" He'd never catch Artie this way. But at least he could keep him in sight.

"Oky-choky," Artie said. "Now you have to turn around. Don't look."

Bert didn't move.

"That's not fair. You promised!" Artie looked ready to cry.

"Oh, all right," Bert said. He turned and counted to ten. Then he looked up. Artie wasn't in sight. Bert took the stairs two at a time. "Stop!" he called. "Artie Houlihan! Whatever you're doing, quit it!"

Bert raced for Artie's room, at the end of the hall. He skidded to a stop and looked in. Artie was on the bed, holding his cat, Fluffy, on his lap.

"That's nice—" Bert began.

The cat yowled.

"Artie, why do you have a paintbrush in your hand?" Bert asked. Then the cat turned its head, and Bert saw the reason.

"Fluffy wants red whiskers," Artie said. "She likes green, too."

He reached for another brush. Fluffy sprang off his lap and out the door.

"You scared her," said Artie. "She scratched me. I got a boo-boo on my thumb. I need to wash it." He jumped off the bed and ran.

Bert reached the bathroom just as Artie pressed his thumb under the faucet. He turned on the water.

"Don't!" Bert said. A cold spray hit him in the face. He wiped his eyes and reached for Artie.

Artie backed up. "I didn't mean to splash you. I was washing my thumb."

Bert groaned and clenched his fists.

"We have to clean up this mess," he said. He handed Artie a sponge. "Come on, you can help."

Artie wiped up some water. Then he wrung out the sponge in the sink. Most of the water went back on the floor. Some of it ended up on Bert's shoes.

"Here, I'll do it," Bert told him. "You just keep out of the way."

Bert wiped up the floor. Then he rinsed out the sponge. He was glad Artie was staying quiet. Bert looked at him. Artie's lower lip was trembling.

"What's wrong?" asked Bert.

"You hurt my feelings," Artie said. "You didn't let me help."

"You were making it worse."

"I don't like you anymore! I want my mommy!"

Bert thought fast. "Artie?" he said. "Would you like a snack?"

Artie wiped his eyes and smiled. "I want candy," he said. "Mommy gives me candy when I get a boo-boo."

Bert rolled his eyes. Mrs. Houlihan had told him not to give Artie candy. She said sugar

made him act wild. The last thing Bert needed was for Artie to get wilder!

"There's candy in the kitchen," said Artie. He squeezed past Bert and scampered down the stairs. Bert was beginning to get tired. Watching Artie was more work than running in a track meet.

Artie was waiting for him in the kitchen. He had two eggs in his hands. "Hey, Bert," he said. "Want to see how I can juggle?"

"Put those back!"

Artie tossed an egg into the air. Bert made a dive for it and caught it in his left hand.

Artie tossed the second egg. Bert stretched his other hand out as far as he could. The egg hit his fingertips, wobbled, and fell onto the floor.

"Oh no!" he said. Then he noticed that his left hand felt wet. He looked down. Egg white and yolk were dripping through his fingers onto the floor. "Yuck!"

He threw the broken egg into the garbage. Then he got a paper towel and wiped his hand. It still felt sticky. He tore off another towel. He got down on his hands and knees and wiped up the mess. Suddenly he felt a breeze on his neck.

Artie was on the back porch.

"Hey, Bert," he called. "Want to play hide-and-seek? You're it."

"Come back here," Bert yelled. But it was too late. Artie had already darted into the dark.

Bert grabbed a flashlight from a shelf and dashed into the yard. "Artie," he called. The only answer was a rustle and a giggle.

Bert circled the yard. Shadows looked ready to leap at him. The bushes seemed like crouching monsters.

Bert knew the only monster in the yard was named Artie. Was he behind the garage?

Bert took a step toward it. Suddenly a blinding beam of light shot down from the sky. Bert crouched and pressed his hands over his eyes. But he couldn't shut out the light.

Then, just as suddenly, the light vanished. The spots faded from in front of his eyes. Bert looked up—and gasped. Just overhead, so close he could almost touch it, was a circle of colored lights. The lights turned slowly at first, then more rapidly. The silence was eerie.

With a faint *whoosh,* the circle of lights flew up. It disappeared behind a line of trees. Bert shook his head.

"Wow!" he whispered. "I don't believe it! I think I just saw a UFO!"

2

A Search

"Nyah–nyah. I was in the toolshed. You didn't find me!"

"Huh?" Bert said. He looked around.

Artie was grinning and hopping up and down. "I won, I won," he chanted.

"Did you see it?" Bert asked.

"See what?"

"The flying saucer! Did you see it?"

"There aren't any flying saucers," said Artie. "They're just pretend."

"But it was right here, a big circle of lights that turned. It flew off that way. Are you sure you didn't see it?"

"Naw," Artie said. "I didn't see anything. And I was right here, too. You're just making up a story. That's not right. Let's play another game!"

"Okay," Bert said, taking Artie's arm. "But we're playing *inside* the house."

Bert was quiet on the drive home from Artie's house. And he didn't tell Mr. Houlihan about seeing the UFO.

When he got into the house, everyone was asleep. He called the Lakeport police and told them what he had seen. "Come downtown tomorrow morning," an officer said. "You can give Detective Peters the details then."

Before he left the house early the next morning, Bert told his mother about the UFO. Then he stopped at Nan's room. She was awake and feeling much better. He quickly told her what had happened at the Houlihans' the night before.

"We'll talk more about it when I get back," he said, and left for the police station.

Bert told his story to Detective Peters. When he had finished, the police detective looked up from his notepad. "You say these colored lights turned in a circle?" he asked.

"Not exactly," Bert said. "It was more like they were along the edge of a disk. The disk was turning."

"Uh-huh. And they were so bright they blinded you. Is that right?"

"No, first came a bright white light. Then it went off, and I saw the colored lights."

Detective Peters checked his notes. "No one else reported seeing this thing last night."

"But I really—"

Detective Peters held up his hand. "Lieutenant Pike talks about you Bobbsey kids," he said. "He has a lot of respect for you. If you say you saw something, you did. But without more to go on, there's not much we can do."

"What if I try to find out more about it?" Bert said.

Detective Peters chuckled. "You go right ahead. And if you learn more about your lights, let us know."

Bert's next stop was the *Lakeport News.* His mother worked at the paper part-time. She had called her office earlier that morning. A reporter named Jack Oldfield was expecting him.

Oldfield listened to Bert's story.

"Who else saw this UFO?" he asked.

"No one," Bert admitted. "But I did see it."

"Of course you did," Oldfield said. "But on stories like this, we like to have more than one witness."

Bert understood what Oldfield meant. He

didn't believe Bert. He thought Bert was making the story up.

Arguing wouldn't convince people. What he needed was more evidence. But how would he find it?

At home he told Nan, Freddie, and Flossie about his interviews. "Oldfield thought I was just some kid who'd seen too many movies," he said.

"What we need is proof," Nan said.

"We could find out what Bert saw," said Flossie. "Then they'd know he was telling the truth."

"Sure, let's go investigate," said Freddie. "Maybe we'll see the aliens!"

"You can stay home and do that," Bert said. Nan and Flossie laughed. The Aliens was the name of the rock group Nan and Bert played in.

Freddie looked puzzled. Then he caught on. "Not them," he said. "Real aliens, with ray guns and stuff."

"You kids finish your lunch," Mrs. Bobbsey said. "You can investigate later."

After lunch the Bobbsey twins set out on their bikes. The Houlihans lived in a hilly area just outside town. It took the Bobbseys about twenty minutes to get there.

"How come," Flossie said, panting, "going uphill is hard but downhill is easy?"

"Simple," Bert replied. "It's the law of gravity."

Before Flossie could ask what that meant, Artie came running toward them.

"Hi," he said. "I was playing in the yard. Mommy saw it was you. She said I could come say hello."

"Hello, Artie," the twins said.

"Did you come to play with me? I have a bike, too. Can we ride around in the driveway?"

Bert shook his head. "We're here on business, Artie," he said. "We're investigating the flying saucer I saw last night."

"Investimating?"

"We want to look around," Nan explained. "Maybe we can find out what it was."

"Can I go too? I want to help. Please, can I?"

Bert looked at Nan. She nodded.

"If your mom—" Bert began to say, then stopped. Artie was running up the driveway to ask.

"What are we looking for?" Flossie asked.

"Yeah," added Freddie, "and where do we look?"

"I don't *know* what we're looking for," Bert said. "Anything that might be a clue."

"As for where," said Nan, "we know the UFO didn't land in Artie's backyard. But maybe it landed nearby. Which way did it go?"

"Over that way." Bert pointed to the woods behind the house.

"Then let's start looking up there, okay?"

Artie came running back, with a big smile on his face. "Mommy said I can go with you," he announced.

"That's nice," Nan said.

Bert groaned.

The Bobbseys found a path and started walking up through the woods. Artie ran ahead, hid behind bushes, and jumped out to scare Flossie. He tried to tie up Freddie with the headphone cord from Bert's tape player. He chased squirrels and threw pebbles at tree trunks. Then he ran back holding a stick. "Look," he cried. "A Cosmic Crusaders power sword!"

Freddie took the stick and raised it in the air. "I have the power . . ." he said in a deep voice.

"Where are we going?" Artie asked. When Bert told him, "Up that way," and pointed, he seemed happy. But a few moments later he asked, "Why?"

"To look for clues," Nan said.

"What's a clue?" Artie asked.

"Something to help us figure out what Bert saw in the sky last night," she replied.

"Oh." After a short silence, Artie said, "I have a book about airplanes at home. Maybe that would help."

Nan laughed. "Thanks, ·Artie," she said. "But that's not the kind of help I meant."

Bert dropped back behind the others. Were they wasting their time? he wondered. It was just a guess that the UFO might have landed up this way. It could have flown on for hundreds of miles. And even if it *had* landed, that didn't mean any evidence had been left behind.

"Look!" Freddie shouted up ahead. He sounded scared.

"Hurry, Bert," Flossie cried.

Bert ran like the wind. He stopped when he saw Freddie, Nan, Flossie, and Artie. They were standing in a clearing, looking at the ground.

"What is it?" he asked.

"I don't know," Freddie said. "Look." He stepped aside.

The grass was pressed down and blackened. It looked as if it had been burned by a giant, fiery foot.

3

Clues from Space

Bert stared at the burned grass.

"What do you think left that?" Nan asked.

"I don't know," Bert said. "But I don't want to meet it after dark."

"I knew I'd find a big clue," said Freddie.

Flossie turned and walked away. If Freddie could find a big clue, so could she.

A few feet away she saw another patch of black grass. She dashed over to it. She walked around it. Then she squatted down to look more closely at it.

Now she could see something she'd missed when she'd been standing. A line in the grass stretched from her spot to Freddie's. It looked as if something heavy had pressed it down.

Still squatting, she turned completely

around. It looked as if there was another, fainter, line alongside the first. But she couldn't be sure.

Flossie stood up. Two giant footprints and a long, straight mark in between. It reminded her of something—

"Yikes!" she cried. The others looked over at her.

"What's wrong?" asked Bert.

"Look what I found." She pointed to her spot and the two long marks in the grass.

"That's terrific, Flossie," said Nan. "But why were you scared?"

"I was wondering what made those tracks. And then I got it! You remember Freddie's T-shirt?"

"Those tracks aren't from an Indian in a canoe," Freddie said.

"Not that T-shirt, silly! The one with the dinosaur. It's standing up on two enormous feet and balancing on a big, heavy tail. And it's got claws as long as my arm and about forty zillion teeth."

Freddie's eyes got wider. "Tyrannosaurus rex," he said. "The fiercest dinosaur of all!"

"And then I thought," Flossie said, "what if the crew of Bert's UFO were dinosaurs?"

"I don't know about dinosaurs," Nan said. "But let's fan out and look for more clues."

She started across the clearing. With each step she looked carefully at the ground. Bert, Freddie, and Flossie, spaced ten feet apart, were doing the same.

Artie grabbed the tail of Nan's shirt. "I'll help you," he said. "I'll look for clues."

"That's okay, Artie, you can stay—" But when Artie heard her say *okay,* he ran off toward the woods. If only I had some rope, Nan thought, I could tie it to his belt as a leash. That wouldn't help much, though. I'd still have to hold it all the time.

But to her surprise, Artie scurried back to her. "Here's a clue, Nan," he announced. He held up a shiny rock. "You can have it."

"Let me explain something, Artie," she said. She knelt down and looked into his eyes. "A clue isn't something that was always here, like a rock or a stick. It's something somebody left here by mistake."

"Like a mitten?"

"Sure," she said. "Or a soda can, or even a footprint. Something that might help us figure out who was here and what he was doing."

"I get it," said Artie. He dashed away again. Nan straightened up. Had she checked the area in front of her or not? She couldn't remember. To be safe, she scanned it again.

"Look, Nan, I found another clue!" Artie ran

up and handed her a cardboard coffee cup. "Somebody left it here, right?"

"I guess so," Nan said. She took the cup and looked it over. It was in good shape, so it hadn't been lying around very long. It said "Cup 'n' Saucer Diner" on the side.

"Is it a clue?" asked Artie.

"It might be, sure."

"Good," he said. "I bet I can find lots more." He ran off. Nan hoped no one had tossed a bag of garbage in the clearing. Artie would probably bring all of it to her, piece by piece.

She was on her hands and knees, looking at some marks in the dirt, when Artie jumped onto her back.

"Giddyap," he said.

"Artie, get off!" Her neck hurt where he was grabbing her. "I'm not playing now."

"Later?" he said.

"Okay, later! Now please get off."

As Artie slid off, his foot dragged across the marks she had been looking at. Her first real clue of the afternoon, gone forever.

"Artie . . .!" she said.

He gave her a big smile. "I got lots more clues," he announced.

"That's okay, Artie," she said. "You can keep them."

"No, no, these clues are for you. They're a present."

He picked up a brown paper bag and emptied it. A candy-bar wrapper, a matchbook, a soda can, the lid of a yogurt container, and an empty flashlight battery package lay scattered before her.

"See?" he said. "Lots of clues. Which one do you want?"

Nan reached for the matchbook. Matchbooks had helped the Bobbsey twins solve more than one mystery. But this one didn't give the name of a fancy restaurant or hotel. It simply showed a smiling face with the words, "Have a nice day."

"Sure," she muttered. "The same to you!"

"Huh?" said Artie.

"Nothing." She looked over his other finds. The candy bar, soda, and batteries were all national brands, sold by the millions. No help there. But the yogurt was a brand she'd never heard of before. She put the lid back in the bag with the rest of the stuff.

At the far edge of the clearing, Freddie saw a faint path into the woods. He looked around. Flossie and Bert were still searching the ground. Nan was in the middle of the clearing, looking at something Artie was holding.

"I'm going this way," Freddie called. He went into the woods.

After the bright sunlight of the clearing, the woods were dark and gloomy. Freddie tried to walk silently. But every step made the dead leaves on the path rustle.

He stopped and listened hard. Had he heard another rustling sound? Was it an echo? Whatever it was, it had stopped when he had.

He straightened his shoulders and took a deep breath. Then he started up the path again. But he couldn't get rid of his feeling. Something in the woods was following him. He looked around. Nothing.

A few steps farther on, the path opened onto a rough dirt road. Freddie wondered if he should follow it. He took out a nickel, tossed it in the air, and missed.

"Rats," he muttered. He bent over to pick up the nickel.

His hand stopped. In the dirt near the nickel was a tire track. It looked too narrow for a car and too wide for a bicycle. It led off the road into the woods.

He straightened up. "Hey, you guys," he called. "Look what I found!"

The others came running. Soon they were on

their knees in the dirt road. They examined the tire print. Then Flossie said, "Maybe a big snake did that."

Artie's eyes grew round. "Where's the snake?" he asked.

"It's a tire print," Bert said. "Wish I had my Rex Sleuther plaster kit. I could—" He pulled a pad and pencil out of his pocket.

Freddie wandered down the road, looking for more tracks. He heard a motor. It sounded like an airplane. But this airplane was coming closer, fast.

Suddenly, a motor scooter roared into view from around the curve.

Freddie jumped to the side of the road. The rider's face was hidden behind a black helmet and visor. He didn't slow down. "Look out!" Freddie yelled.

Bert, Nan, and Flossie ran for safety as the motor scooter hurtled toward them. But Artie stood in the middle of the narrow road. He was too scared to move. In another instant he would be run down!

4

A Soda in a Flying Saucer

Nan had to do something, fast. Artie stood frozen, right in the path of the scooter. His eyes looked as big as pies.

Nan took a quick, deep breath and darted into the road.

She reached down and scooped Artie up. He seemed to weigh a ton as she jumped to the other side of the road.

Her foot hit a loose rock, and she fell into a ditch. Artie landed on top of her. Her ankle hurt, but for once she didn't care. Artie was safe.

The scooter skidded to a stop. A spray of pebbles pelted Nan's face and arms.

The rider raised his visor. He had a red face.

His pale eyes bulged as if they might pop out.

"What kind of idiots are you?" he shouted. "What were you doing in the middle of the road?"

"Taking a walk," said Nan, trying to look innocent. She stood and brushed herself off, then helped Artie up. His face was pale; and he was shaking.

"In these woods? That's not very smart," the man said. "People don't come into these woods if they can help it."

"What do you mean?"

"It's not even safe to talk about it," he said. "But some things in these woods don't want to be disturbed. People who bother them don't last long."

Bert stepped up beside Nan. "Thanks for the warning," he said. "Maybe you should drive slower. Other people use the road, too."

"Kids," the man muttered. He snapped his visor down, revved up the scooter engine, and roared away. Pebbles and dust sprayed everywhere.

Bert coughed and wiped his eyes. "Nice guy," he said. "Very friendly."

"Always kind to children and dogs," Nan added with a grin.

Artie scowled. "I don't like him," he said. "I think he's mean!"

"Never mind him," Bert said. "He won't bother you again."

"I want a drink of water," Flossie said.

"Let's take Artie home," Bert said. "We can all use a break."

Artie's father was in the backyard mowing the lawn.

"Daddy!" Artie shouted, running toward his father. Mr. Houlihan cut the motor.

"I found a lot of clues. And a man on a scooter nearly knocked me down."

"What?" said Mr. Houlihan. He turned to Nan.

"We were on a dirt road up that way," she explained. "A man on a scooter was going too fast. But he didn't hurt anyone—he just scared us a little. Do you know who he is? He has pale blue eyes and a red face."

Mr. Houlihan nodded. "I know who you mean," he said. "Felix Usher. He's been renting the Stockton cottage for the last few months. That's just the other side of the hill."

"I don't like him," Artie repeated.

"You shouldn't talk that way about people," his father said. "Anyway, Usher keeps to himself. I see him now and then, hiking or on that scooter. But he never stops to chat."

"Are there any stories about these woods?" Bert asked.

"Stories? You mean like buried treasure?" Mr. Houlihan shook his head and smiled. "Fred Stockton always said his house used to be a hideout for smugglers and gangsters. That's before my time, though. I never heard they left treasure behind. They probably spent it all."

The Bobbseys were on their way home when Nan saw a diner up ahead. She grinned and pedaled fast to catch up to Bert. She called to him, and he stopped. A moment later Freddie and Flossie joined them.

"What's wrong?" asked Freddie.

"Nothing," Nan said. "I thought we should stop for a soda."

"Why here?" Freddie asked.

Nan gave him a sly smile. "We can't pass that up, can we?" she asked. She pointed to the sign over the restaurant: Flying Saucer Diner.

Freddie grinned back. "I guess not," he said.

They parked their bikes and went in. The place had a lunch counter with stools, six or eight booths, and not much else. The closest thing to a flying saucer was the video game.

"Wow," Freddie said, "Space Invaders! I'll buy you a game."

"Not now," Nan said. She gave Freddie a warning look. "Let's sit at the counter."

They were the only customers. A man with

a big, dark beard came over. "Four colas, please," Nan said.

After he brought their sodas, Nan reached into the paper bag she was carrying. She pulled out the coffee cup Artie had found. "Is this from here?" she asked the man.

He looked at it and frowned. "No," he said. "Or, rather, yes."

"What do you mean?" asked Bert.

"This *was* the Cup 'n' Saucer Diner," he replied. He had an accent Nan had never heard before. "When I bought it from Mr. Stockton two years ago, I wanted a more modern name. Something to catch the eyes of people who go by. But new signs cost money. So I changed part of the old one."

"I get it," Bert said. "You kept the Saucer part and changed the *Cup 'n'* to *Flying*. That was smart."

The man smiled. "Very smart idea, from a very smart friend of mine. I even saved the *n* and made a *y* out of the *p*."

"But what about the coffee cups?" Nan said. "You couldn't change those."

"No. I used up the old ones. Then I bought these." He reached over and got a cup to show them. It had a drawing of a UFO on the side, and the words, *Flying Saucer Diner, Lakeport— Best Coffee in the Universe.*

"Very up to date," the man said. "Did you hear the radio today? Some boy saw a flying saucer right here in Lakeport. Maybe they came for my coffee!"

Flossie nodded. "This is my brother Bert. He's the one who saw the flying saucer!"

Bert's face turned bright red.

"That's wonderful," the man said. He handed the coffee cup to Bert. "Here. Keep it for a souvenir."

"Thanks. But where do you think *this* one came from?" Bert asked.

The man shrugged. "Not from here," he said. "Not now. I have been using the new design for over a year."

He smiled and added, "Maybe someone invented a time machine! Excuse me, I have things I must do. Please call if you want something. My name is Chuck."

He vanished into the back.

The twins lingered over their sodas. They talked about the marks in the clearing, Artie's escapades, and their close encounter with the scooter. Finally, when Flossie finished chewing up all her crushed ice, they got up to leave.

"That's funny," Bert said as they walked outside. "Look."

A tape cassette was sitting on the seat of his bike.

"Maybe you dropped it and somebody picked it up," said Freddie.

"I didn't bring a tape," Bert said. "I've been using the radio." He popped the strange cassette into his recorder, put on the earphones, and listened. His eyes narrowed. After less than a minute, he pushed the rewind button.

"Here," he said, holding up the earphones. "Lean close and you can all hear it."

The voice on the tape sounded as if it were coming from a mixed-up computer. Nan had trouble understanding the words. But the message was clear. She felt as if a cold wind had just swept across the diner parking lot.

"You saw nothing," the chilling voice said. "You will say nothing. You will remember nothing. If you do not obey, you and your family will never forget what will happen to you. You have been warned!"

5

Questions—But No Answers

Bert pushed the stop button and rewound the tape. "How do you like that?" he said.

"I don't like it at all," said Nan. "Whoever left it knows who we are and where we were."

"And we don't know anything about him," Flossie added.

Bert frowned. "We don't even know it's a *him*," he said. "It might be an *it*."

"Don't say that," Flossie cried. "You're giving me chills."

"Look!" Freddie said. "Down there by Bert's foot—it's another tire track!"

The two boys knelt down to examine it. "This mark's a lot like the one up in the woods," Bert said.

"It looks exactly the same to me," Freddie said.

"Whoever left that tape came here on those tires," Nan added.

Bert started to sketch the tire marks. Flossie watched for a few moments. Then she said, "I don't think so."

"Think what?" Bert said.

"The tape," she replied. "I think Chuck put it there."

"Aw, c'mon," said Freddie.

"No, I mean it! He knew we were here. And I told him about Bert. I think he's from the UFO. Maybe he's the captain of it."

"That's an interesting idea, Floss," Bert said. "Except for one thing. How would he know we'd come to the diner?"

"Well . . ." she said slowly. "But wait! Remember? He went in back. He was there a long time while we were drinking our sodas. He could have made the tape then. And put it on your bike."

Bert folded his sketch of the tire mark. He put it in his shirt pocket along with the cassette. Chuck didn't look like an alien. But he'd keep Flossie's idea in mind. It was too soon to rule anything out.

"We'd better be getting home," he said, climbing on his bike.

Nan shook her head. "You guys go ahead," she said. "I want to check something out. I'll see you later."

Bert and the younger twins came racing up the driveway. Then Bert stopped short. His mother was sitting on the front porch with a woman Bert had never seen before. Mrs. Bobbsey waved to the twins.

Bert parked his bike and went up the steps. Freddie and Flossie rode on back to the garage.

"Bert, this is Lenore Bainbridge," Mrs. Bobbsey said. "She'd like to talk to you about what happened last night."

"Hello, Bert," the woman said. "It's nice to meet you."

"Hi," Bert answered.

"I heard about you on the radio," she went on. "So I drove right over to Lakeport."

"Really?" he said. "Where from?"

"It doesn't matter." Ms. Bainbridge seemed irritated. "The point is, I'm writing a book about people who've seen UFOs. I'd like to ask you some questions. While your memories are still fresh."

"Okay." Bert perched on the porch railing and swung his feet back and forth.

"I'll leave you two, then," Mrs. Bobbsey said. "There are things to do in the house."

For the next ten minutes, Lenore Bainbridge asked Bert one question after another. What colors were the lights he had seen? Which way had they revolved and how fast? What direction had the UFO gone when it left? Bert didn't remember, or hadn't noticed, half the things she wanted to know.

Finally she closed her notebook.

"Ms. Bainbridge?" Bert said.

"Call me Lenore."

"Did anybody else ever see what I saw?"

She hesitated, then said, "I really can't say."

Bert persisted. "But there've been lots of UFO sightings, haven't there? Did anybody you've talked to see the colored lights? The ones that went around in a circle?"

"N-no, I haven't heard that description before."

"But you've talked to a lot of people who've seen UFOs?"

"Quite a few, yes. I wish we could talk longer, but I have a lot of errands. Thanks for your help." She stood up and left the porch.

Bert stood on the steps with his hands in his pockets and watched her get into her car. It was red and had out-of-state license plates. As she drove off, he took down her license-plate number. Something about Ms. Bainbridge didn't seem quite right.

*   *   *

"Oh, *please,* Freddie," said Flossie. "I know Chuck's in this. We'll hang around and keep an eye on him. We'll probably solve the whole mystery this afternoon!"

"I don't want to ride back to the Flying Saucer now," Freddie said. He was lying on the grass with his hands behind his head. "We just got home. I'm tired."

"We can play Space Invaders," Flossie said.

"Well . . . maybe later on."

"I'll pay if we go now."

"Yeah?" He sat up. "How many games?"

Flossie checked her pockets. "Uh, a couple," she said.

"It's a deal," he said, jumping to his feet. "Get the bikes. I'll tell Mom where we're going."

When they walked into the diner, the owner was talking to a bearded man. Chuck looked surprised to see them again so soon. Flossie and Freddie headed for the video game. Flossie put a quarter in the machine and Freddie began to play.

The bearded man said something in a foreign language and stood up. He carried his coffee cup to a booth in the corner. A couple of minutes later another man came in. He greeted

Chuck in what sounded like the same language. Then he joined the first man at his booth.

Flossie wandered around the diner. Gradually she drew closer to the corner booth. The men stopped talking. She gave them one of her cutest smiles. The man with a beard said something that made the other man laugh.

"Hey, Flossie," Freddie called. "It's your turn."

She went back to him. "Why did you do that?" she asked in a low voice. "I might have heard something. It might have helped us solve the mystery."

"Oh, sorry," Freddie replied. "I forgot. Anyway, it's your turn. Bet you can't beat my score."

A few minutes later Chuck came over to watch. Flossie got nervous and missed some shots.

"You are very lucky kids," Chuck said. "You are growing up knowing about computers and such. Where I come from, we have no computers, no Space Invader games. These things are like magic to us."

"Where *do* you come from?" asked Flossie. She wondered what she would do if he answered Mars.

"A small country in Europe," he said. "My

friends are from there also. We get together to talk of the old times."

"Come on, Flossie," Freddie said. "Put in another quarter."

She reached into her pocket and turned it inside out. "I'm out of money," she confessed. "We'll have to go home."

"Here," Chuck said, holding out a coin to Freddie. "Play a last game as my guest."

Nan put her bicycle in the rack on the sidewalk. So far she'd been to three supermarkets and two small grocery stores. None of them sold the brand of yogurt she was looking for. Nobody had even heard of it.

The manager at the grocery on Main Street had suggested she try the health-food store. "You'll find all sorts of peculiar food there," he had said.

She studied the window of the health-food store. There were dozens of kinds of honey, and cereals she'd never heard of. In front of them was a rack of books about eating right. And in the corner was a small sign advertising the yogurt! "*Made with genuine imported cultures,*" it said.

She had finally found the right store! Just then the door opened and a man walked out.

He unwrapped a candy bar, tossed the wrapper on the sidewalk, and turned in her direction.

It was Felix Usher.

He saw Nan and stopped. For a moment he stared at her. Then his face grew redder. He strode up to her and grabbed her arm.

"You!" he said. "Are you following me? I warn you, it's not smart to get me angry!"

6

ZAP!

"Let go of me," Nan shouted. She tried to pull her arm away. Usher held it tighter.

"I asked you a question!" he said in a voice full of menace. "You'd better answer if you want to stay healthy."

"I don't know what you're talking about!"

The door to the health-food store opened and the clerk looked out. "Hey, is that guy bothering you?" he demanded.

Nan twisted her arm and tried to back away. "Make him let go!" she said.

The clerk started toward them. "Come on, sir," he said. "Leave that little girl alone!"

Nan didn't like being called a little girl. But she liked the result.

"All right," Usher growled. He let go of her arm so abruptly that she almost fell. "But remember what I said."

He stalked away. A few moments later, his scooter roared up the street.

"Thanks," said Nan.

"Don't mention it," the clerk replied. "Hey, do you know that guy? I'd keep out of his way if I were you. If you ask me, he's a little nutso."

Bert was in his room on the third floor of the Bobbsey house. He was reading a Rex Sleuther comic, looking for ideas. Flossie tapped on the door and came in.

He tilted his chair back and said, "What's up?"

"Will you come with me to the candy store?" she asked.

"Now?" Bert answered.

"Please. I really, *really* want some of those jelly bunnies."

"Well . . ." He let his chair fall forward and stood up. "Okay. Who's paying?"

Flossie's face turned pink. "I'm broke," she said in a low voice.

"I should have guessed," Bert said.

"I did have money," she protested. "But I spent it all on the investigation." She told Bert about the trip to the diner.

"That's different," said Bert. "I'll treat. Come on."

When they walked into the candy store,

Bert's heart sank. Some kids he knew from school were looking at the afternoon edition of the *Lakeport News*. And one of them was Danny Rugg. Danny enjoyed being mean to other kids.

Danny looked up and saw him. "Look, guys," he said. "Here he is, right out of the newspaper. Hey, Bobbsey, did you see any green men?"

Andy Somers put his palm over his mouth and went, "Oooo-eeee-oooo!"

"Lay off," Bert muttered. His cheeks felt hot, and he was sure his ears were red.

"Bert Bobbsey," Andy said in a deep voice, "call home!"

"You know where that is, don't you?" Danny said. "The Planet of the Apes!"

"You leave my brother alone," Flossie cried.

"Hey, look, they're not all apes," Danny said. "This one's a little monkey."

Bert balled his fists and took a step toward Danny.

"Okay, you kids," the cashier called. "Take your arguments outside."

"Come on, Bert," said Flossie. "We've got better things to do than listen to those guys."

On the sidewalk, Bert glanced at his watch. "I'd like to take another look at those marks you found," he said. "Okay? You never got your candy."

Flossie grinned at him and got on her bike. "That's all right. I'll get some exercise instead. Race you to the Houlihans'!"

They left their bikes at the Houlihans' and walked up the path to the clearing. The sun was low, and everything looked different. The lines in the grass were clear. Bert thought he could see other, fainter, lines as well.

He had an idea. From the ground the lines seemed faint and scattered. But how would they look from the sky? He had read that all kinds of marks show up in satellite photos. How would this clearing look from twenty thousand miles up? Would the lines show? Maybe they would form a pattern. Or spell a message! But in what language, from what planet?

He took Flossie on a slow walk around the clearing. Every few feet he stopped and scanned the area. Sometimes he stooped down. Sometimes he got up on tiptoe. Sometimes he just stood in one spot, moving his head from side to side.

All at once he said, "What's that?"

Flossie peered at the tall grass. "Where?" she asked. "I don't see anything."

He put his hand on her shoulder. "No, listen!"

They both concentrated. Bert was starting to think he'd been mistaken. Then he caught it again.

"It's the motor scooter," Flossie said. "I think it's coming this way."

Bert shook his head. "It's stopped."

"I want to go home," said Flossie. "I'm hungry."

Bert sighed. It really was time to be getting home. In the Bobbsey family, working on a mystery excused a lot of things, but not missing a meal.

"Okay," he said. "Let's go."

They jogged down the path and retrieved their bicycles. They were about to ride onto the road when they heard a car start nearby. Bert and Flossie ducked behind a tree. A red car drove slowly by.

Bert couldn't see the driver's face. But he knew the license plate. It was the car Lenore Bainbridge had been driving. Had she come out here to look at the spot where Bert had seen the UFO? Or was she following Bert and Flossie?

Freddie cranked the pedal until his bike's rear wheel was spinning fast. Then he leaned over and put his ear near the wheel. All he heard was a hissing sound. That was okay. The spokes caused it, slicing through the air. But the faint high-pitched squeal he noticed earlier was gone.

He turned his bike right side up and wiped his hands on a rag. All fixed!

Nan rode up the driveway and stopped next to him. "How did you do this afternoon?" she asked.

"I won two games!"

"Congratulations," Nan said. "You played tennis?"

"Are you kidding? Space Invaders!" He saw that she still didn't understand. "Flossie and I went back to the Flying Saucer Diner to play."

"I get it. Well, maybe we should all sit down and tell what we found out."

"We can't," he said. "Flossie dragged Bert off to the candy store. Hey, I know what!"

"What?" Nan asked.

"We could look at that road again, the one through the woods. It wouldn't take long. I think I know a shortcut to it."

Nan shrugged. "Okay, lead on."

Half a mile before the Houlihan house, Freddie turned onto a side street. It was marked Dead End. He waited for Nan.

She looked at the sign. "You do know where you're going, don't you?"

"Uh-huh. A kid in my class used to live in that house over there. He showed me all kinds of secret paths and stuff."

"Okay," Nan said, "but you'd better not get us lost."

After the pavement ended, a dirt road continued into the woods. A hundred yards in, it began to climb. They had to get off and walk their bikes.

"Look," Freddie said a little later. He was pointing to a tire track in the dust.

"It's the same as the one we saw before, isn't it?" Nan said. "We must be up behind the Houlihans' now. Where do you think the path to the clearing is? Over— What's that!"

An eerie, high-pitched whine came from the woods to the left of the trail. It grew louder and higher. Nan thought her eardrums would burst. Freddie grabbed her arm.

The sound stopped. A sudden flash of light blinded Nan. She shut her eyes. She could still see the afterimage of the flash.

"Nan!" Freddie cried. "Look!"

She opened her eyes and blinked. Then she blinked again, in disbelief. A tree right near them had just burst into flames!

7

The Flying Monster

Freddie spun his bike around and made a running jump onto the seat. He flew down the bumpy dirt road. Nan raced after him.

She caught up to him and shouted, "Whoa!"

"Did you see that?" They both came to a halt. "Somebody shot a ray gun at us! I bet it was some kind of laser!"

"I wonder," Nan said. "Didn't it take an awfully long time to fire after we heard that noise? And we were an easy target, standing there. So why did it miss us and hit the tree?"

"I don't know," replied Freddie, shuddering. "But I'm glad it did. I wouldn't want to go up in flames like that tree."

"You know, I'd like a closer look at that tree. There's something phony about this."

"Are you crazy?" Freddie cried. But Nan had

already started up the hill again. Shaking his head, Freddie followed her.

Nan left her bike on the road and jumped a ditch to examine the scorched tree. "Come see," she told Freddie.

"Here, look at this thin line in the bark," she continued. "It goes all the way around. And look, all the burn marks fan out from it and go up the trunk."

"So the flames started from here?"

"That's what I think. Somebody fastened a flare to the tree with wire. Then he pretended to shoot at us with a ray gun."

"I get it. But how did he know we were coming?"

"I don't know. Not many people use this road. Maybe it was set off by an electric eye or something."

"Oh." Freddie's face twisted with concentration. "Listen, Nan, wouldn't real aliens have real ray guns? Why would they need to fake it?"

"I don't think they would," she replied.

"Then they're not aliens at all! They're humans pretending to be aliens!" He paused. "But if Bert didn't see a UFO, what *did* he see?"

"That," said Nan, "is a very interesting question. Come on, we'd better get home."

* * *

After dinner the four Bobbseys gathered in the living room. Freddie described the ray-gun attack. Then Nan told what they'd found when they returned to the scene.

Bert snapped his fingers. "Lenore Bainbridge! Flossie and I saw her driving away. She must have just come from setting up the attack!"

"What time was that?" asked Nan.

Bert hesitated. "I didn't notice," he said.

"That's okay," Nan said. "I didn't write down what time that tree caught on fire, either. I was too busy trying to catch up to Freddie."

"I beat Nan down the hill," Freddie put in. "I bet I went thirty miles an hour."

"Maybe it wasn't that woman who did it," said Flossie.

"It had to be, Floss. We saw her."

"I know, but remember? Before that, we heard a sound like a motor scooter."

"That's right, we did."

"Usher!" Nan looked angry. "I should have known!" She told them about the scene at the health-food store.

"Maybe *he* set the ray-gun trap," Flossie said. "He sounds pretty nasty."

Maybe he and Lenore Bainbridge are in on it together," Freddie pointed out.

Bert said, "Tomorrow we'll see what we can find out about both of them."

"Don't forget Chuck," said Flossie. "I still think he's suspicious."

"I won't," Bert promised. "But we've done all we can for now. Who wants to watch *The Comet Patrol?*"

Flossie went to bed happy. She'd had pizza for dinner and chocolate ice cream for dessert.

Later, though, she woke up suddenly. The house was dark and quiet. Her heart was pounding the way it did when she'd had a bad dream.

She closed her eyes and rolled onto her side. Then she heard an eerie whistling sound. It got louder and softer, louder and softer. It was as if something was coming close, then moving away.

Flossie sat up and looked around. The window was a lighter patch in the darkness of her room. She got up and walked over to it.

Fog was drifting in gray wisps across the yard. The lights of Lakeport reflected off the low-hanging clouds.

Flossie shivered. On TV, scenes like this always meant something scary was about to happen.

The whistling sound grew louder, then stopped. She looked down into the yard. Something was down there. Something that didn't belong. Something that didn't belong on Earth! It glowed in the darkness, a pale unhealthy green. It looked like an enormous head. Two glowing eyes stared up at her.

The head began to move.

Slowly, silently, it drifted up toward her window. Flossie clutched at the curtains. She wanted to back away, to run, but her legs wouldn't obey her.

The head came closer, then closer still. Flossie couldn't breathe. The head looked as though it might come right through the glass into her room. It darted toward the house. She screamed.

As if it had heard her, the head raced up into the mist and vanished. Nan, Bert, Freddie, and her parents ran into the room.

"What is it?" Mrs. Bobbsey asked, wrapping Flossie in her arms.

"There was something outside. It glowed in the dark. And it came up to the window. Then I yelled, and it went away."

Nan went to the window, opened it, and looked out. "There's nothing there now," she reported.

Flossie was getting over her fright. "I think I

scared it away," she said. "I yelled pretty loud."

"You sure did," Freddie said. "I thought the house was on fire."

Flossie ignored him. She told the others what had happened in more detail. When she mentioned the whistling sound, Nan looked thoughtful.

"Okay, everybody," Mr. Bobbsey finally said. "Back to bed. You can try to find out what it was in the morning."

The twins searched the yard before breakfast. It didn't take long. The grass had been mowed the week before, and there weren't many places for a clue to hide.

Nan checked the flower beds along the back of the house.

She almost missed the clue. Between two of the bricks that edged the flower bed was a crumpled piece of foil. She picked it up, unfolded it, and sniffed. Then she touched it with her fingertip.

The others came over. "Nothing," said Bert.

"Me, neither," Flossie reported.

"Floss, are you sure—" Freddie started to say.

Nan interrupted him. "I found this," she said, holding up the foil. "And I think I know what Flossie's visitor was. Let's go inside."

She led them into the pantry and closed the

door. When their eyes adjusted to the darkness, they saw a glowing green hand. Flossie let out a yell.

"What?" Bert exclaimed. He turned on the light.

Nan grinned at them and wiggled her fingers. "Glow–in–the–dark paint," she explained. "Somebody painted a helium balloon. Then they made that whistling noise that woke Flossie up, and let the balloon drift up toward the window."

Flossie stuck her head out from behind Bert.

"I bet the bad guys came after me because they knew I'd track them down. And they wanted to scare me off before I did. But it won't work!" she said.

Nan shrugged. "Maybe. But whoever did it probably just picked a window at random. I don't think he cared which of us he scared."

"He, or she," Bert said. "It might have been Lenore Bainbridge."

Nan nodded. "Or more than one person."

"I still suspect Chuck," Flossie said.

"But he doesn't know about computers," Freddie argued. "He couldn't have made that weird-sounding tape Bert found."

"He and his friends speak a strange language," Flossie pointed out. "He said they're from Europe, but how do we know they aren't from Mars?"

"Don't worry," Nan promised. "I won't forget about Chuck. And I won't be scared off by a balloon."

One thing Nan did forget was her promise to take care of Artie that afternoon. She was surprised when the Houlihans' car pulled into the Bobbsey driveway. Artie jumped out and ran into the house.

He was in high spirits. In minutes, he piled Freddie's toys in the middle of his room. Then he emptied Flossie's dresser in hers. Then he crawled under Nan's bed and refused to come out. She finally lured him downstairs by offering to make him a peanut butter sandwich with a face in it.

After the snack, Flossie and Freddie took Artie exploring in the basement.

Nan went into the study. She powered up her mother's computer and used the modem to get into the data base at the *Lakeport News*. After entering Mrs. Bobbsey's password, she asked for a search on the key words "flying saucer."

Only one item turned up. It was about the grand opening of the Flying Saucer Diner last year. The new owner, Constantine "Chuck" Milios, talked about how different Lakeport was from his old home in Europe.

Nan chuckled. So much for Flossie's idea that Chuck was a Martian.

She cleared the screen and keyed in "UFO." This time she was luckier. There had been half a dozen UFO sightings in the past few weeks. She copied the locations and plotted them on a map. They led in a straight line from Lakeport. But where did they start?

The words on the screen scrolled upward and new words appeared.

"WARNING . . . EARTH . . . WARNING . . . EARTH," they said. "POWER . . . OURS . . . WARNING . . . TARGET . . . TARGET . . . EARTH."

Nan's shout brought Freddie, Flossie, and Artie up from the basement. The twins read the message. "Where did it come from?" asked Flossie.

"Someone sent it through the modem," Nan explained. "Get Dad, I want him to see this."

Flossie left the room, and Artie came over to the desk.

"Hi, Nan," he said. "I missed you. Can I type on your 'puter?"

Nan grabbed for Artie's hand. But she wasn't fast enough. The moment he touched the keys, the message faded from the screen. The clue was gone!

8
Aliens?

Nan stared at the blank computer screen. "Oh, no," she said with a groan. Then she realized she could call up "UFO" again. Maybe the threat would reappear.

But when she got to the end of the list of sightings, nothing happened. The message was definitely gone.

Just then, the phone rang. Nan switched off the modem and answered it.

"Nan? It's Mrs. Houlihan. I'll be later than I expected. Can Artie have dinner with you?"

"That's fine," Nan replied. Then she had an idea. She crossed her fingers. "Mrs. Houlihan? We promised Artie we would look at his collection of Cosmic Crusaders characters. When you come to get Artie, would you mind taking us home with you? My mom or dad could pick us up later."

"I'd be glad to," Artie's mother said. "He adores being with you kids. You know, this UFO business is great fun for him. But to tell you the truth, it's getting on my nerves. It's becoming a real bother."

"Really? How?"

"Well, this will give you an idea," she said. "This morning a woman came to my door at eight o'clock. I was just giving Artie his breakfast. She asked if she could sit in my backyard for a while. She wanted to beam mental messages into space."

Nan laughed. "What did you tell her?"

"That my son needed to play there. She marched back to her little red car and drove away in a huff. She didn't go far, though. Later I saw her car parked along the road. She was probably sitting in a field. Communicating with creatures from another planet."

"A red car?" Nan said. "What did she look like?"

"Oh, let me see. In her mid-twenties, I suppose. She had straight brown hair and brown eyes."

Nan frowned. That sounded like Bert's description of Lenore Bainbridge. What had she really wanted to do in the Houlihans' yard?

Nan sat in the front seat of the car next to Artie. He demanded that she play eensie-weensie-spider with him the whole trip.

"Look," Bert said, pointing out the window. "Doesn't that motor scooter look familiar?"

"It sure does," Nan replied. "And that looks like the street that leads to the dirt road, too. Right, Freddie?"

"I think so. Yes," he added as they drove past, "that's it."

"Mrs. Houlihan," Nan said, "would you mind letting me off just ahead?"

Mrs. Houlihan slowed down and pulled over to the side of the road.

"I'm going with you," Bert announced.

"Me, too," Freddie and Flossie said at the same time.

"I want to go, too," said Artie. "Please, can I?"

Nan rolled her eyes. "No way," she said. "Bert and I will meet you guys at Artie's house. We'll be there before you know it."

Flossie and Freddie started to argue. But Nan glared at them and they quieted down.

A few minutes later Nan and Bert were hiking up the dirt road. Suddenly Nan put her hand on Bert's arm. She gestured for him to listen. The *putt-putt* of the scooter had stopped.

"He got to where he was going," Nan said softly.

"The clearing?" Bert asked.

"Maybe. Let's go find out."

They walked quietly, in single file. Nan's heart was beating fast, and her mouth felt dry. Usher might come around the next bend. Or he might be watching them from the woods. Or he might be home at the Stockton cottage, cooking his dinner.

They drew close to the scorched tree. Nan felt her shoulders hunch, ready for an attack. Something poked her. She jumped and nearly cried out.

It was only Bert. He put his finger to his lips, then pointed to the left. There, hidden in the bushes, was Usher's motor scooter.

"Come on," Nan mouthed. She tiptoed over to the scooter. Bert was right behind her.

A carrier was attached to the rear of the scooter. She peered in. Then she lifted out a flashlight, a Thermos bottle, and a stack of cardboard coffee cups.

She nudged Bert with her elbow and showed him the cups. Printed on the sides were the words *Cup 'n' Saucer Diner.*

"Let's get out of here," Bert whispered. "He might come back."

Nan fiddled with the flashlight for a moment. Then she put it and the other things back. "Okay," she whispered. "Let's take a shortcut."

"Remember when I found that burnt spot?" Freddie said to Artie. "That was our first important clue." Artie looked at him admiringly.

"I found a burnt spot, too," Flossie said. "And the lines in the grass. Remember those? Bert thought they were very important."

Freddie and Artie didn't seem to hear her.

"Then yesterday," Freddie continued, "Nan and I were attacked. By somebody with a ray gun."

"A ray gun?" said Artie. "Wow! What did you do?"

"He rode away as fast as he could," Flossie said. They still didn't hear her.

"We figured out it wasn't a real ray gun," Freddie said. "And that's the most important clue of all."

"It is not," Flossie protested.

"It is so. Listen, real aliens . . ."

Flossie didn't stay to hear the rest. Freddie had already explained it to her five times.

What made his dumb ray gun so important, anyway? What about the scary monster that had come to her window the night before? Nan figured out that was a fake, too. Wasn't it just as important a clue?

Flossie walked out into the yard, thinking hard. Where could she find a really important clue? Maybe the place to start was the clearing. If the UFO had landed there, it might have left some traces they hadn't found yet.

A little way up the path to the clearing, she stumbled and almost fell. A wire was strung across the path to trip people. She went down on one knee and looked at it. Then she grinned.

The wire was string. And it wasn't even tied. It was just around a couple of bushes. It must be Artie's idea of how to trap an alien.

Flossie left the string where it was and continued up the path. As she got closer to the clearing, she thought she heard voices. She left the path and crept up through the woods. When she was almost at the clearing, she got down on her hands and knees. She wriggled a little further on her stomach. Parting two branches, she looked out into the open space.

She felt as if somebody had just touched her neck with an ice cube. A woman was walking past her, not a dozen feet away. She was describing what she saw. Now and then she paused, then spoke again. It was as if she were answering somebody's questions.

It sounded normal. It didn't look normal, though. The woman was the only person in the clearing. She was talking, and listening, to thin air.

Flossie was sure the woman was talking to the UFO. She sounded as if she were giving it landing directions. Bert and Nan needed to know about this. Right away!

Flossie backed out of her hiding place and got to her feet. She was almost to the path when she stepped on a branch. It cracked under her foot.

"Who's there?" the woman shouted.

When she needed to be, Flossie was a fast runner. She took off down the narrow path, hardly seeming to touch the ground. A shout behind her made her run even faster.

She remembered Artie's trip wire an instant too late. It snagged her left ankle. She crashed to the ground.

The fall dazed her. She knew she had to get up. She had to keep running. But she couldn't. She had twisted her ankle. When she tried to stand up, it hurt. She bit her lower lip to keep from yelling.

She slumped back to the ground and tried rubbing the ankle. The pain seemed to be getting better. But she knew she couldn't run. She wasn't even sure she could walk.

Someone was running down the path. More than one somebody. Maybe the woman had beamed down some aliens to capture Flossie.

What could she do to escape? She thought hard and fast. She couldn't do anything! It was all over!

9

Return of the Saucer

The footsteps came closer. Flossie tried once again to stand. Her ankle hurt too much. If she couldn't run, could she hide?

She began to crawl off the path. It was hard work. Her shoelace tangled in a bush. The more she tried to tug it loose, the more tangled it became.

The aliens were just around the bend now. No time left. She gulped and shut her eyes.

"Flossie!" someone shouted. It sounded like Bert's voice.

She opened her eyes. It *was* Bert. Nan was right behind him.

"What's wrong?" he asked. He knelt down next to her. "Are you okay?"

"I tripped and hurt my ankle."

Bert looked at it. "We saw you running," Nan said. "We called your name, but I guess you didn't hear us."

"Boy, were you going fast," said Bert. "What were you running from?"

"Aliens. I saw a woman up in the clearing. She was talking to somebody who wasn't there. Then I stepped on a branch. She heard me, so I ran. I forgot there was a string across the path."

"Where's Freddie?" asked Nan.

"Back at Artie's house." Flossie scowled. "Talking about how he found all the important clues. I wanted to show I could find some, too."

"Okay," Nan said. "I get the picture. But we're not in a contest, you know. We work together."

"We'll have to carry you to the house," Bert said. "Nan, do you remember how to make a seat with our arms? The firefighters showed it to us at assembly last year."

They had to experiment a few minutes before they got it right. Flossie sat on their interlocked arms and held onto their shoulders. They carried her carefully down the path to the Houlihans'.

Mr. Houlihan met them in the yard. He carried Flossie into the house and put her on the sofa.

Mrs. Houlihan examined her ankle. "It's just twisted," she finally said. "Her doctor may want to see it, but that can wait until tomorrow. For now I'll just soak it in cold water and put an elastic bandage on it. Then I'll call your parents and tell them what's happened."

Nan looked troubled. "If they say they'll come to get us," she said, "would you mind telling them to wait until I call them?"

Mrs. Houlihan seemed surprised. But she agreed to pass on the message.

Flossie was surprised, too. But she knew the signs. Nan was cooking up something. Sure enough, she took Bert aside and started whispering to him.

Flossie watched his face. It went from looking puzzled, to thoughtful, to happy. When Nan was done, he nodded and said, "It's worth a try."

He came over to Flossie. "We'll be right back," he said with a grin. "Don't go anywhere."

"Ooh!" Flossie exclaimed. "I'll get you for that! Where are you going? What's going on?"

He patted her shoulder. "Don't get in an uproar, Floss. I'll tell you all about it later."

He and Nan were gone for a few minutes. When they came back, Nan asked if she could make a telephone call.

Flossie listened hard.

"Hello, Lakeport police?" Nan said. "May I please speak to Lieutenant Pike?" After a pause, she lowered her voice and spoke for a long time.

She hung up, looked at Bert, and nodded. Then she went into the other room and talked to Mr. and Mrs. Houlihan.

"Rats," said Flossie. She was going to miss whatever Nan and Bert were setting up. "I never get to do any of the fun stuff."

"You can help us play," said Artie, heading toward her. He was holding a model car and a train set. Freddie carried a pile of blocks.

Flossie groaned. "That's *just* what I wanted to do."

"*Vrooom,*" said Artie. His black Grand Prix car zoomed along the racing track. Then it smashed into the side of a bridge and fell onto the train tracks below.

"I told you," Flossie said from the sofa. "The bridge has to be wider."

Freddie brought more blocks from Artie's room and began to rebuild the bridge.

Artie shifted his attention to the train set.

The brightly colored wooden cars were held together with magnets. They ran in grooves in the wooden tracks. There were switches, and even a siding with a magnetic crane.

"*Chuff, chuff, chuff,*" Artie said, pushing the train around the curve. He was headed for Freddie's bridge.

"Hey, wait," Freddie said. "Look out!"

"*Whoo, whoo!*"

By itself, the train would have fit under the bridge just fine. Artie's hand didn't. He went on pushing, and the bridge scattered across the floor.

"Now look what you did," said Freddie.

Artie smiled and said, "*Whee!*" He knocked down what was left of the bridge.

Flossie laughed. Freddie looked so angry. "I remember when you used to do that to Bert."

"Now I know why Bert always wanted to kill me," Freddie answered. "Artie's just a little kid." He sighed, looking at Artie. "Tell you what. I'll build something really big for you to knock down, if you leave my bridge alone next time."

"Really, *really* big?" said Artie. "And really tall? Can I help?" He went around the room collecting the blocks and piling them near Freddie.

Three castles and two skyscrapers later,

Flossie looked up and noticed it was dark outside. That surprised her. She'd been having fun watching the boys play. But wasn't it about time to go home?

Nan must have been reading her mind. She and Bert came into the living room. "It's time," she said. But instead of getting ready to leave, she turned off the lights.

"Hey," Freddie said, "we can't see."

"Shh!"

Flossie saw Artie's mother switch off the kitchen lights. She and Mr. Houlihan came into the living room.

"Are we playing a game?" Artie said. "I'm scared."

His mother picked him up and held him in her arms.

After a long, tense silence, Nan said, "We could be wrong, Bert. We're just guessing about—"

"Shhh!"

Flossie strained her ears. The only sound she heard was the refrigerator.

She jumped when Bert said, "There! Everybody come watch!"

"I can't!" Flossie wailed.

"I'll help you," Nan said.

Flossie's pulse was racing as she hopped over to the sliding glass doors.

"There, over the hilltop," said Bert. "See it?"

Flossie looked, and looked again. At first she saw only the night sky. Then she gasped. Just above the horizon, hovering in one place, was a whirling circle of multicolored lights.

"I see it!" Freddie exclaimed. "It's moving!"

He was right. The lights moved slowly toward the house. They were sparkling like a necklace. Closer, and closer still, until the necklace was right above the yard. It seemed near enough to touch.

A beam of white light speared down from the craft. The backyard was as bright as day.

Bert's UFO had come back!

10

Down to Earth

The Houlihans' backyard had become a brightly lit stage. As if by magic, Bert thought, watching from inside the house. The spotlight beaming from the UFO was amazing. But the sparkling circle of lights was the star of the show.

Felix Usher ran into the yard, waving his arms. His eyes looked ready to pop out of his head.

The strange craft floated down, lower and lower. Then two metal runners touched the ground.

"The marks in the grass!" Flossie said. "That's what they were!"

Orange flames flickered in the brightness. The exhaust from the UFO set two small patches of grass on fire. The circling lights slowed down, then stopped moving. For the first time, they all saw the craft itself.

"A helicopter!" Flossie exclaimed. "It wasn't from Mars after all!"

The landing lights went out. Bert saw spots in front of his eyes. The spots changed from white and blue to pale orange, then faded.

The backyard was pitch black for a second. But then light flooded it once again.

This time, there were half a dozen lights, all around the yard. They were bright enough for Bert to read "U.S. Air Force." Someone had painted the words over, but not well.

Usher looked toward the dark house, then toward the lights. He crouched and ran to the helicopter. Two men were inside.

"This is the police," a voice boomed suddenly. "Remain where you are. I repeat, this is the police. Remain where you are. Do not attempt to leave the area."

Nan poked Bert. "That's Lieutenant Pike," she whispered.

Usher looked back in the direction of the voice. Before he could decide what to do, two police officers came into the pool of light. One of them handcuffed Usher. The other motioned the pilot and copilot out of the plane and handcuffed them.

Lieutenant Pike stepped into the light. He looked into the helicopter. Then he turned toward the house. He smiled and made an okay sign.

Flossie let out a gasp. The woman she had seen earlier talking to no one, had just appeared in the yard. As she walked to the helicopter, her lips moved.

Flossie tugged at Bert's sleeve. "Look," she whispered. "She's doing it again. She's talking to the air!"

Bert grinned. "That's Lenore Bainbridge. Look at her belt," he said.

"A radio!" Flossie said. "So that's it! Is she some kind of police officer?"

"I think so," said Bert. "We'll find out for sure pretty soon."

"It was the runner marks that first tipped us off," Nan said.

Two officers had taken Usher, the pilot, and the copilot into town. Lieutenant Pike and Lenore Bainbridge, along with the Houlihans, were listening to Nan.

"Flossie's the one who noticed them," Nan said.

Flossie smiled proudly.

"Then we had the exhaust burns Freddie found," said Bert.

Freddie grinned.

"Uh-huh," Nan said. "Put those together with Bert's description of the whirling lights. It adds up to a helicopter of some kind."

"Hold on," Mr. Houlihan said. "I've seen lots of helicopters, of all kinds. The thing they all have in common is how noisy they are. What Bert saw was totally silent."

"That's right," Bert said. "You didn't hear it just now, did you?"

"No," Mr. Houlihan said with a smile. "It didn't make enough noise."

"But that's just—" Bert began. Then he realized Mr. Houlihan was teasing him. "Right," he said. "That's the point."

"Either it wasn't a helicopter at all," Nan explained, "or it was a very advanced one—specially designed to be silent. When I studied the list of UFO sightings in the past few weeks, I plotted them on a map. They started near an Air Force base."

"Simple," Freddie said. "But what about the ray gun, and the thing that came up to Flossie's window?"

"That was Usher's work both times," said Bert. "He wanted to keep us imagining flying saucers and aliens from outer space. That way we wouldn't think of helicopters."

"A stolen helicopter," Lenore Bainbridge said. "And top secret, too."

Lieutenant Pike cleared his throat. "Lieutenant Bainbridge is with Air Force security," he said. "She's been working on this case."

"That's right," she said. "The thieves wouldn't dare fly the XH-8 in the daytime. But anyone who noticed it at night would think it was something new and strange. In other words, a UFO."

"So you went on a UFO hunt," Nan said.

"I came to Lakeport the minute I heard about Bert's sighting," Lieutenant Bainbridge said. She chuckled. "I made a mistake, pretending to be a writer. If I'd known about you kids, I would have put together a better cover story!"

"I thought you were from Mars," Flossie confessed. The others, including Lenore Bainbridge, laughed.

"But Felix Usher," Mrs. Houlihan said. "He seemed like such an ordinary man. Whatever made you suspect him?"

Nan reached over and rumpled Artie's hair. "Your son found some of the most important clues," she said. "You see, Usher was always snacking and littering. If he hadn't been a litterbug, he might not have been caught."

"The yogurt lid," Flossie said.

"Uh-huh. Artie found a lid from an unusual brand of yogurt. The only place that carries it is a health-food store. It's also just down the street from a cycle shop. Probably where Usher got his scooter. That's not proof, but it *is* a link."

"What about the paper coffee cup?" asked Freddie.

"That was a terrific clue, once we figured it out," Bert said. He turned to Lieutenant Pike.

"The cup was freshly used," he explained. "But it came from a diner that doesn't exist anymore. The Cup 'n' Saucer."

"That was the name of Fred Stockton's place," said Mrs. Houlihan.

Bert nodded. "That's right. And Usher was living in Stockton's cottage. We figured Stockton had kept a supply of the old cups at home. Usher found them and used them."

Nan said, "We found some in the carrier of his scooter, with a Thermos of coffee."

"Exactly what happened here tonight?" Artie's mother asked. "I saw it all, but I still don't understand."

Nan glanced at Bert. His grin said that she should tell the story.

"Well," she began, "we saw Usher's motor scooter up in the woods. The Thermos and cups were in it. So was a powerful flashlight.

We guessed his gang was going to test the helicopter tonight."

Bert broke in. "Nan took the bulb out of his flashlight. He couldn't signal the helicopter."

"He might have had spare batteries. But he probably wouldn't have a spare bulb," Nan said with a grin.

"That was a smart move," Lenore Bainbridge said.

"There's not much else to say," Bert continued. "We rigged the Houlihans' flashlight in the backyard, to fool the helicopter into coming down here. Then we called Lieutenant Pike to be ready for it."

"And I alerted Lenore Bainbridge," Lieutenant Pike added.

"And I've alerted the Air Force," she said. "Thanks to the Bobbseys."

"I'll bet it was Mr. Usher that sent us that message on Mom's computer!" Flossie exclaimed. "He tried to scare us away, but we were too smart for him. Right?"

"Well . . ." Nan said sheepishly. "We weren't *that* smart. Bert called home to tell Mom and Dad about our plan—"

"Yeah," said Bert. "And they said there wasn't really a warning message. Uh—we kind of messed up the *Lakeport News*'s computer files on UFOs."

"We were reading bits and pieces of their files," Nan continued. "Not a warning. Mom is a little upset with us."

"Anyway," said Bert, "we solved the case. If Artie hadn't run into the yard that night, I wouldn't have been there with the flashlight. Then none of this would have happened."

Artie had fallen asleep on his mother's lap. At the sound of his name, he woke up.

"Bert?" he said. "You want to play a game? You want to play Cosmic Crusaders?"

Bert rolled his eyes. "Tomorrow, Artie," he said. "We'll play tomorrow."

NANCY DREW® MYSTERY STORIES By Carolyn Keene

THE TRIPLE HOAX—#57	69153	$3.50	_____
THE FLYING SAUCER MYSTERY—#58	65796	$3.50	_____
THE SECRET IN THE OLD LACE—#59	69067	$3.50	_____
THE GREEK SYMBOL MYSTERY—#60	67457	$3.50	_____
THE SWAMI'S RING—#61	62467	$3.50	_____
THE KACHINA DOLL MYSTERY—#62	67220	$3.50	_____
THE TWIN DILEMMA—#63	67301	$3.50	_____
CAPTIVE WITNESS—#64	62469	$3.50	_____
MYSTERY OF THE WINGED LION—#65	62681	$3.50	_____
RACE AGAINST TIME—#66	69485	$3.50	_____
THE SINISTER OMEN—#67	62471	$3.50	_____
THE ELUSIVE HEIRESS—#68	62478	$3.50	_____
CLUE IN THE ANCIENT DISGUISE—#69	64279	$3.50	_____
THE BROKEN ANCHOR—#70	62481	$3.50	_____
THE SILVER COBWEB—#71	62470	$3.50	_____
THE HAUNTED CAROUSEL—#72	66227	$3.50	_____
ENEMY MATCH—#73	64283	$3.50	_____
MYSTERIOUS IMAGE—#74	69401	$3.50	_____
THE EMERALD-EYED CAT MYSTERY—#75	64282	$3.50	_____
THE ESKIMO'S SECRET—#76	62468	$3.50	_____
THE BLUEBEARD ROOM—#77	66857	$3.50	_____
THE PHANTOM OF VENICE—#78	66230	$3.50	_____
THE DOUBLE HORROR OF FENLEY PLACE—#79	64387	$3.50	_____
THE CASE OF THE DISAPPEARING DIAMONDS—#80	64896	$3.50	_____
MARDI GRAS MYSTERY—#81	64961	$3.50	_____
THE CLUE IN THE CAMERA—#82	64962	$3.50	_____
THE CASE OF THE VANISHING VEIL—#83	63413	$3.50	_____
THE JOKER'S REVENGE—#84	63426	$3.50	_____
THE SECRET OF SHADY GLEN—#85	63416	$3.50	_____
THE MYSTERY OF MISTY CANYON—#86	63417	$3.50	_____
THE CASE OF THE RISING STARS—#87	66312	$3.50	_____
THE SEARCH FOR CINDY AUSTIN—#88	66313	$3.50	_____
THE CASE OF THE DISAPPEARING DEEJAY—#89	66314	$3.50	_____
THE PUZZLE AT PINEVIEW SCHOOL—#90	66315	$3.95	_____
THE GIRL WHO COULDN'T REMEMBER—#91	66316	$3.50	_____
THE GHOST OF CRAVEN COVE—#92	66317	$3.50	_____
THE SAFECRACKER'S SECRET—#93	66318	$3.50	_____
THE PICTURE PERFECT MYSTERY—#94	66311	$3.50	_____
NANCY DREW® GHOST STORIES—#1	46468	$3.50	_____

and don't forget...THE HARDY BOYS® Now available in paperback

Simon & Schuster, Mail Order Dept. ND5
200 Old Tappan Road, Old Tappan, NJ 07675
Please send me copies of the books checked. (If not completely satisfied, return for full refund in 14 days.)

☐ Enclosed full amount per copy with this coupon
(Send check or money order only.)
Please be sure to include proper postage and handling:
95¢—first copy
50¢—each additonal copy ordered.

☐ If order is for $10.00 or more,
you may charge to one of the
following accounts:
☐ Mastercard   ☐ Visa

Name _____ Credit Card No. _____

Address _____

City _____ Card Expiration Date _____

State _____ Zip _____ Signature _____

Books listed are also available at your local bookstore. Prices are subject to change without notice.   NDD-25

THE HARDY BOYS® SERIES By Franklin W. Dixon